First published in 2012 by
The Puppet Company Ltd
Units 2–4 Cam Centre
Wilbury Way
Hitchin
Herts
SG4 0TW

www.thepuppetcompany.com

ISBN: 978-1-908633-02-6

British Library Cataloguing-in-Publication Data
A catalogue record for this book is available
from the British Library

Printed in China

Jack and the Beanstalk

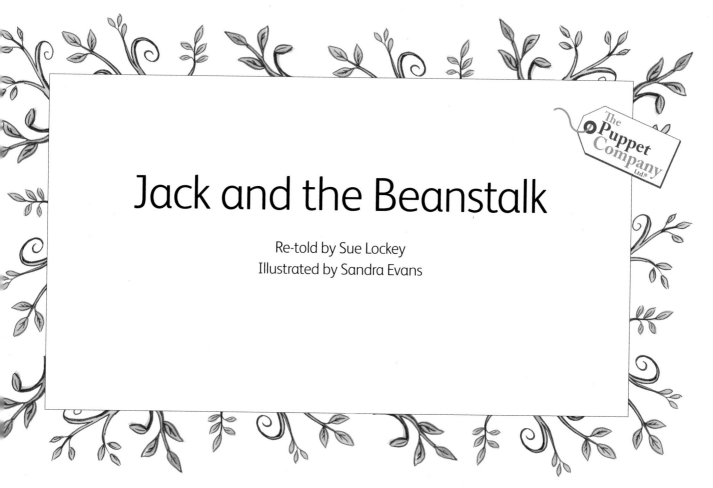

Jack and the Beanstalk

Re-told by Sue Lockey
Illustrated by Sandra Evans

The Puppet Company Ltd®

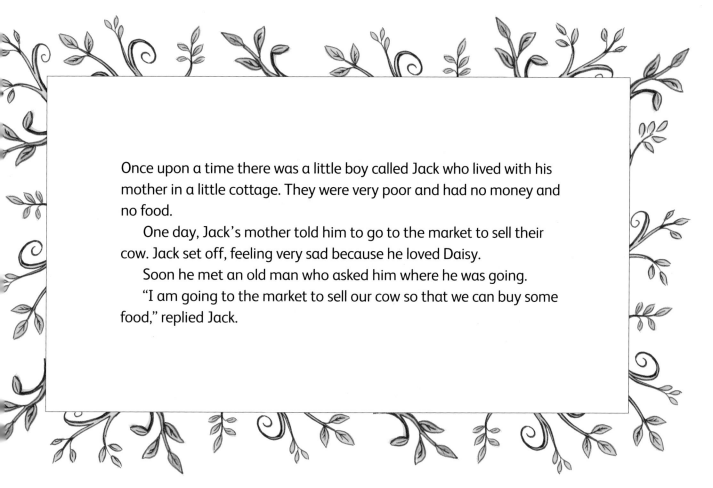

Once upon a time there was a little boy called Jack who lived with his mother in a little cottage. They were very poor and had no money and no food.

One day, Jack's mother told him to go to the market to sell their cow. Jack set off, feeling very sad because he loved Daisy.

Soon he met an old man who asked him where he was going.

"I am going to the market to sell our cow so that we can buy some food," replied Jack.

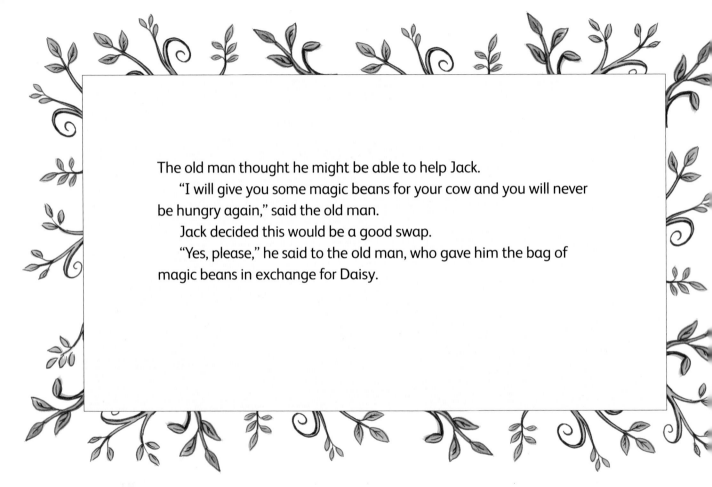

The old man thought he might be able to help Jack.

"I will give you some magic beans for your cow and you will never be hungry again," said the old man.

Jack decided this would be a good swap.

"Yes, please," he said to the old man, who gave him the bag of magic beans in exchange for Daisy.

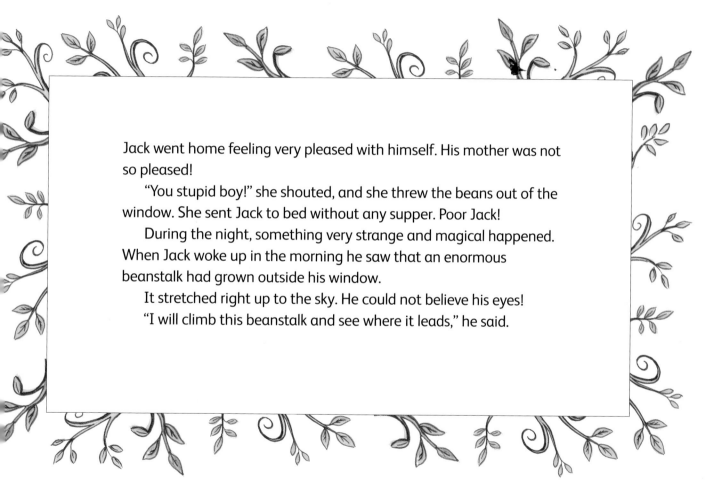

Jack went home feeling very pleased with himself. His mother was not so pleased!

"You stupid boy!" she shouted, and she threw the beans out of the window. She sent Jack to bed without any supper. Poor Jack!

During the night, something very strange and magical happened. When Jack woke up in the morning he saw that an enormous beanstalk had grown outside his window.

It stretched right up to the sky. He could not believe his eyes!

"I will climb this beanstalk and see where it leads," he said.

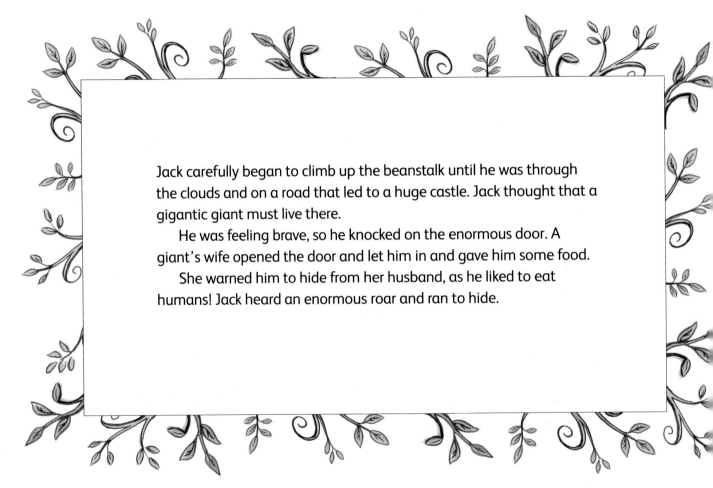

Jack carefully began to climb up the beanstalk until he was through the clouds and on a road that led to a huge castle. Jack thought that a gigantic giant must live there.

He was feeling brave, so he knocked on the enormous door. A giant's wife opened the door and let him in and gave him some food.

She warned him to hide from her husband, as he liked to eat humans! Jack heard an enormous roar and ran to hide.

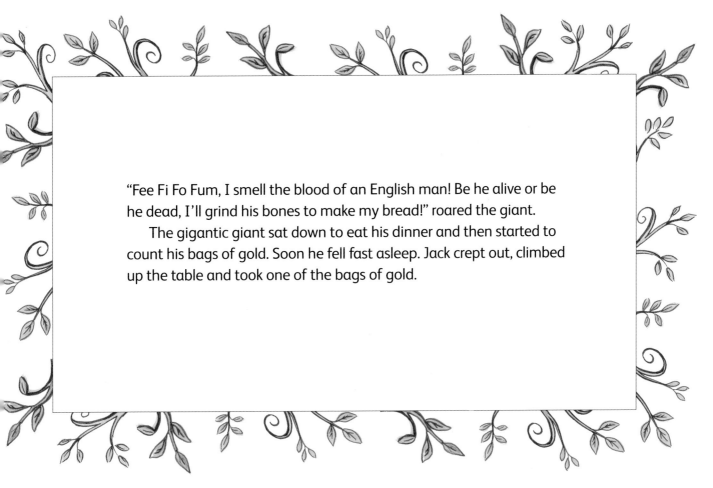

"Fee Fi Fo Fum, I smell the blood of an English man! Be he alive or be he dead, I'll grind his bones to make my bread!" roared the giant.

The gigantic giant sat down to eat his dinner and then started to count his bags of gold. Soon he fell fast asleep. Jack crept out, climbed up the table and took one of the bags of gold.

Jack ran out of the castle and climbed down the beanstalk as fast as he could. His mother was very pleased, and for a long time they lived very well.

When they had spent all the gold coins, Jack decided to climb up the beanstalk again.

When he got to the top, he went to the castle and the giant's wife let him in. Jack heard an enormous roar and ran to hide.

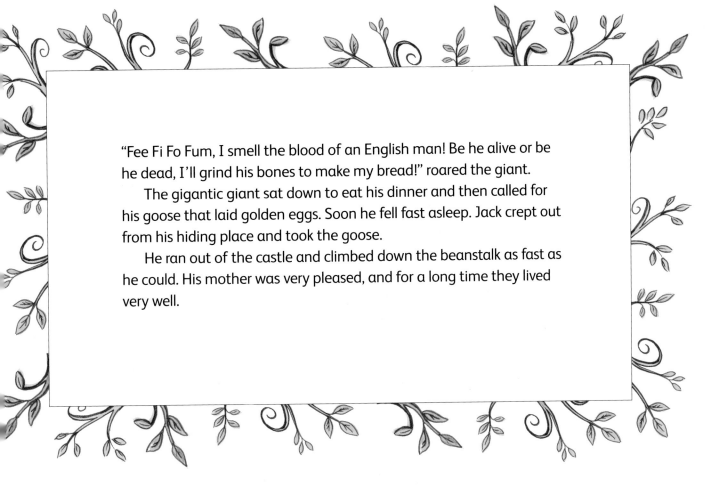

"Fee Fi Fo Fum, I smell the blood of an English man! Be he alive or be he dead, I'll grind his bones to make my bread!" roared the giant.

The gigantic giant sat down to eat his dinner and then called for his goose that laid golden eggs. Soon he fell fast asleep. Jack crept out from his hiding place and took the goose.

He ran out of the castle and climbed down the beanstalk as fast as he could. His mother was very pleased, and for a long time they lived very well.

After a while, Jack decided to climb up the beanstalk again. When he got to the top, he went to the castle and the giant's wife let him in. Jack heard an enormous roar and ran to hide.

"Fee Fi Fo Fum, I smell the blood of an English man! Be he alive or be he dead, I'll grind his bones to make my bread!" roared the giant.

The gigantic giant sat down to eat his dinner and then commanded his beautiful golden harp to play. Soon he fell fast asleep. Jack crept out from his hiding place and took the golden harp.

Suddenly the giant woke up. With a mighty roar, he chased Jack out of the castle and down the beanstalk. Jack was very scared!

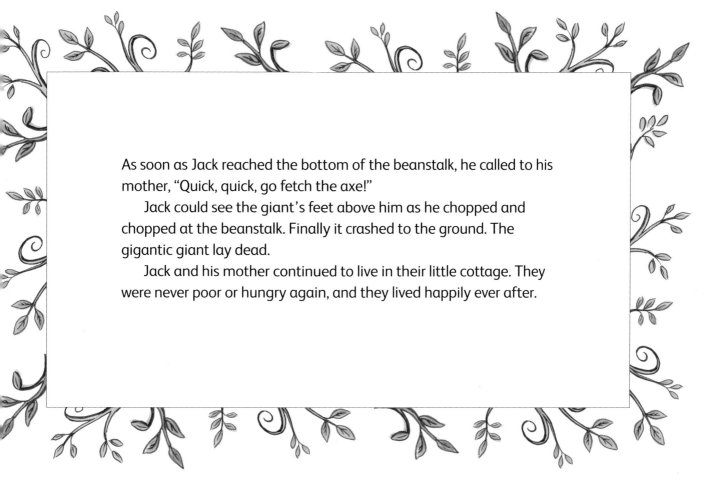

As soon as Jack reached the bottom of the beanstalk, he called to his mother, "Quick, quick, go fetch the axe!"

Jack could see the giant's feet above him as he chopped and chopped at the beanstalk. Finally it crashed to the ground. The gigantic giant lay dead.

Jack and his mother continued to live in their little cottage. They were never poor or hungry again, and they lived happily ever after.